WHAT'S IN A...

LOG?

Tracy Nelson Maurer

ROURKE PUBLISHING

www.rourkepublishing.com

www.rourkepublishing.com

Photo credits: Cover and Page 3 © Neil Webster; Page 4 © Alan Gleichman; Page 5/6 © gregg williams; Page 7 © dragon_fang; Page 8 © Maryunin Yury Vasilevich; Page 9/10 © Intraclique LLC; Page 11/12 © Kovalvs; Page 13 © Brandon Seidel; Page 14 © Ron Kacmarcik; Page 15 © Chris Alcock; Page 16 © goran cakmazovic; Page 17/18 © Gabor Ruff; Page 19 © prism68; Page 20 © Catalin Petolea, jtyler; Page 21 © Ultrashock, Milena, Adam Gryko, Chin Kit Sen; Page 22 © Ron Kacmarcik, Maryunin Yury Vasilevich, Gabor Ruff; Page 23 © Kovalvs, Intraclique LLC, goran cakmazovic

Editor: Jeanne Sturm

Cover and page design by Nicola Stratford, Blue Door Publishing

Library of Congress Cataloging-in-Publication Data

Maurer, Tracy, 1965-
 Log / Tracy Nelson Maurer.
    p. cm. -- (What's in a--?)
 Includes bibliographical references and index.
 ISBN 978-1-61590-281-1 (alk. paper)
 ISBN 978-1-61590-520-1 (soft cover)
 1. Forest animals--Habitations--Juvenile literature. 2. Tree trunks--Juvenile literature. 3. Coarse woody debris--Juvenile literature. 4. Animals--Habitations--Juvenile literature. I. Title.
 QL112.M328 2011
 591.73--dc22
                        2010009259

Rourke Publishing
Printed in the United States of America, North Mankato, Minnesota
033010
033010LP

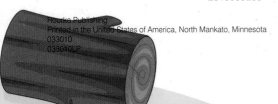

Rourke Publishing

www.rourkepublishing.com - rourke@rourkepublishing.com
Post Office Box 643328, Vero Beach, Florida 32964

A log is full of life.

Can you guess what's in a log?

rat-a-tat-tat

rat-a-tat-tat

What pecks for insects under the bark?

5

A woodpecker.

chomp chomp
chomp

What uses logs to build a dam?

7

A **beaver.**

What grows like
buttons on the bark?

Mushrooms.

What quietly hunts for insects?

A **hedgehog.**

What armored animal
burrows in a log?

13

An **armadillo.**

What spins a web
in the branches?

15

A **spider.**

crunch

crunch

crunch

What eats lunch inside?

A **chipmunk.**

What helped build
a fort with logs?

My brother and me!

What else visits a log?

Picture Glossary

 **armadillo** (AR-ma-DILL-oh): The armadillo has sharp claws that can tear apart logs. It eats bugs, plants, and other food.

 **beaver** (BEE-vur): A beaver eats plants, such as the woody part of trees. It uses mud and logs to build its home, called a dam.

 **chipmunk** (CHIP-muhnk): A chipmunk eats nuts, seeds, and other plant parts. It may store food for winter in its burrow.

hedgehog (HEJ-hog): A hedgehog is a small mammal known for its spiny hair which is stiff, like a fingernail, and hollow.

mushrooms (MUSH-roomz): Mushrooms have been used for medicine and food. Some wild mushrooms are poisonous.

spider (SPY-dur): A spider spins a sticky silk web to catch insects or other spiders for food.

Index

armadillo 14

bark 5, 9

beaver 8

chipmunk 18

dam 7

fort 19

hedgehog 12

insects 5, 11

mushrooms 10

spider 16

woodpecker 6

Websites

www.kids.nationalgeographic.com

www.eol.org

www.inaturalist.org

About The Author

Tracy Nelson Maurer likes to explore the area near Minneapolis, Minnesota, where she lives with her husband and two children. She holds an MFA in Writing for Children & Young Adults from Hamline University.